X

Wonderful Alexander
and the Catwings

A Richard Jackson Book

Also by
Ursula K. Le Guin
and S. D. Schindler

CATWINGS
CATWINGS RETURN

Ursula K. Le Guin

Wonderful Alexander and the Catwings

Illustrations by

S. D. SCHINDLER

ORCHARD BOOKS · NEW YORK

Orchard Books, 95 Madison Avenue, New York, NY 10016

Manufactured in the United States of America
Book design by Mina Greenstein
The text of this book is set in 14 point Cloister.
The illustrations are pen-and-ink drawings and wash,
reproduced in combined line and full color.
10   9   8   7   6   5   4   3   2   1

Library of Congress Cataloging-in-Publication Data
Le Guin, Ursula K., date.
Wonderful Alexander and the Catwings / Ursula K. Le Guin ;
illustrations by S. D. Schindler.
p.   cm.
"A Richard Jackson book"—Half t.p.
Summary: After being rescued by a flying cat, Alexander the cat
decides to make good on a promise to do wonderful things.
ISBN 0-531-06851-X.   ISBN 0-531-08701-8 (lib. bdg.)
[1. Cats–Fiction.]   I. Schindler, S. D., ill.   II. Title.
PZ7.L5215Wo   1994   [Fic]—dc20   93-49397

To the BEAN from Ursula

To SPOOKY, FURBALL, and FIFI,
my visual reference cats

— S. D. S.

THE FURBY FAMILY lived in great luxury. They had a fine house in the country, with a fireplace, feather beds, and a cat door. The Caretaker fed them delicious meals twice daily and dropped tidbits for them when she was cooking. On weekends the Owner came in a little red car and stayed a night or two, and petted them, and gave them treats of sardines to eat and catnip mice to play with.

Mr. Furby was quite stout, and slept a good deal. Mrs. Furby, whose mother was a Persian, had an exceptionally beautiful, long, silky, golden coat. The Furby children were all very plump and lively—especially Alexander.

Alexander was the oldest kitten, the biggest, the strongest, and the loudest. His little sisters were quite tired of him. He was always bossing them around, and when they played chase-tail he knocked them over and sat on them. But Mr. and Mrs. Furby and the Caretaker and the Owner looked on and laughed and said, "Alexander's all boy! Nothing frightens Alexander!" When a little old poodle came to visit, and Alexander walked right up to it and scratched its nose, they laughed and admired him more than ever. "He's not even afraid of dogs! Alexander is wonderful!"

Alexander was sure they were right. He liked to think of himself as Wonderful Alexander. And he intended to do wonderful things.

So one winter day when all the other Furbies were sleeping in a warm pile on a feather bed, Alexander went out the cat door all by himself and set off to explore the world.

He believed that the world ended at the

garden fence. He was surprised to discover that there was another side to the fence. On the other side was a field, and in the field lived some very large black-and-white strangers, who said "Moo!" to him.

"That's a silly thing to say," said Alexander. "You should say Mew, not Moo!"

The big strangers just looked at him and sighed and went on chewing.

Alexander trotted on past them with his tail held high. He knew that the world didn't end with this field, because in the distance he could see tall trees. He headed for the trees. Slipping under another fence, he found himself on a narrow, dark plain that stretched as far as he could see to the left and to the right. The trees were just on the other side of it, and he trotted bravely forward.

He heard a strange purring noise, far away. He wondered if it might be lions. His father had told him about lions. The noise grew from a purr to a deep roar. It must be lions, Alexander thought, but he would not be frightened—until he looked to the right, and saw a huge truck rushing at him, its headlights like terrible staring eyes. He crouched in panic. The wind of the truck as it roared past rolled him over and over in the stinging gravel thrown up by its giant wheels. Bruised and half-blinded, he staggered to his feet, and saw another monster truck bearing down on him. He scrambled forward, fell into the ditch at the road's edge, clambered up the other side, and ran as fast as he could to the dark shelter of the trees.

He was deep in the forest before he stopped, out of breath. He sat down to lick his bruised shoulders and arrange his golden fur, which was dirty with oil and dust. Trees stood all about him, and birds talked up in the branches.

"I really am discovering the whole world!" Alexander thought. And he walked fearlessly on, until a new noise made him stop and listen.

Somebody was barking.

"I'm not afraid of dogs!" Alexander thought. "I'll scratch their noses!"

And on he went—until out of the bushes two tall hounds came leaping, with bright eyes and sharp white teeth.

The next thing he knew, Alexander was looking down at those sharp white teeth, and the dogs' bright eyes were looking up at him—far, far up—at the top of a pine tree.

"Dumb kitten," one hound said to the other. "Come on. Let's find a rabbit!" And they wandered off, grinning.

Evening was coming on, and few birds flew now through the cold, still air. Way up above the birds, Alexander clung to the tree with all his sharp little claws, his fur on end, his eyes round, his ears listening, listening. There was no sound of the dogs, or of anything else.

"I guess I'll climb down now and go home," Alexander said to himself. And he looked down.

Down, down.

He could hardly see the ground.

He looked around. Nothing but tree-tops—and all the treetops were below him. He had climbed to the top of the tallest tree in the forest. And if he let go—if he moved one paw—he might fall.

He held tight.

"Somebody will come and get me," he thought.

A cold wind blew, and the tree swayed back and forth.

"Don't do that!" Alexander said to the tree.

The cold wind ruffled his fur, and he shivered. He tried not to shiver, because he thought he might shiver himself loose from the tree.

"The Caretaker will look for me," he thought. But he knew he had gone a long way from home.

"Father will know where I am," he thought. But he knew that when he left the house, his father had been sound asleep.

"Mother will find me!" he thought, and held on.

But his mother did not come, and the night did.

It grew very dark. A few dry flakes of snow drifted down. Alexander was so cold he couldn't feel his paws. Was he still holding on to the tree? He was so tired, and so hungry! It was long past dinnertime. Maybe they were out calling for him, wandering about the garden, calling, "Kitty, kitty, kitty! Alexa-a-ander!"

"Mew!" he said, as loud as he could. "Mew! Mew! I'm here! It's me, Alexander! I'm up here!"

The forest was silent. Nobody answered him. Only out of the darkness came a great, silent shape on silent wings. The Owl had heard him crying. She flew around him, saying nothing.

Alexander saw her beak and her terrible talons. He knew it was no use trying to scratch her nose. But he puffed himself up as big as he could and hissed at her. "Go away!" he said fiercely. "Scram!"

The Owl gave a low chuckle and flew off.

Just below Alexander a small branch stuck out from the tree. Very slowly and carefully, shaking with cold and fear, he loosened his claw-hold and eased himself down till he could sit on the branch where it joined the tree trunk. There he huddled, holding on. He dared not cry for help again. It was black night now, but the snow clouds parted and the half-moon shone through now and then. And there Alexander waited all night long.

2

As LIGHT CAME into the sky, the birds began to talk softly to each other. They flew about in the trees, but kept well away from Alexander. Desolate and half-frozen, Alexander watched them and thought, "If only I could fly!"

Whenever he tried to look down at the ground again, he grew dizzy, and dug his claws into the branch. He could not make himself climb down. He was afraid.

"Mew," he said in a thin, shaky voice, as the sun rose. "It's me. Help me, please!"

He looked over the treetops, wondering who could ever find him deep in the forest and high in a tree. He did not know where his home was. As he looked all round for a glimpse of its roof above the trees, he saw a bird flying straight towards him, coming nearer and nearer.

He knew that a cat shouldn't be afraid of a bird. But last night he had seen the Owl.

Alexander made himself as small as he could, and said nothing.

But the bird kept coming straight at him, looking at him, and its eyes were round and golden, like the Owl's eyes. Alexander shut his own eyes and tried as hard as he could to look like a pinecone.

The branch jiggled a little.

Alexander opened one eye.

On the very end of the branch sat a strange, black bird. A strange, black bird with whiskers, and four paws, and a long tail. A bird that purred.

"Are you a catbird?" Alexander whispered.

The strange bird looked at him and smiled.

"Who are you?" Alexander asked.

"Me!" said the strange bird.

"My name is Alexander Furby," Alexander said. "I climbed this tree yesterday. I spent the night here. I'm not quite sure which way is the right way down."

The strange bird pointed a paw down at the ground.

"I know," Alexander said. After a while he said, "I'm scared."

The strange bird walked along the branch, sat down right next to him, and began to wash his ear. It felt very warm and pleasant, as if he were home with his little sisters and they were all washing one another and purring and playing chase-tail.

"You're a *cat*!" Alexander said.

"Purr, purr," said the stranger.

"But you have wings!"

"Purr, purr," she said, smiling.

"Can't you talk?"

The stranger lashed her tail a little, looking sad.

"Well," said Alexander, "I can't fly."

"Purr, purr," said the stranger, and washed his other ear with her pink tongue. She looked a little older than Alexander, but she was smaller—a pure black kitten with golden eyes and beautiful, furry black wings.

"I wish I *could* fly," Alexander said. "Because although I am a wonderful climber up, I am not a wonderful climber down."

The black kitten looked thoughtful. Then, folding her wings, she crept carefully down the tree trunk to the next branch below. As she went, she looked back at Alexander over her shoulder, as if saying, "Watch: see where I put my paws." Then she waited on the lower branch.

Alexander took a deep breath and started down, doing just what she had done. In a few moments he was sitting beside the black kitten on the lower branch, his heart beating wildly.

One branch at a time, step by step and paw by paw, she led him down and down the tree, always showing him the way and waiting for him. At last in a wild scramble they both came down the last bit head first and landed thump! thump! in the moss at the foot of the tree.

They were so pleased with themselves that they had a game of chase-tail right there. But soon Alexander discovered that he was tremendously hungry and thirsty. He followed his new friend, who went half-trotting and half-flying through the bushes to the bank of a little stream. The edges were icy, but Alexander broke the ice with his paw, and both of them had a long drink.

The black kitten sat watching him, as if to say, "Now what?"

"I should go home," Alexander said. "My family will be very upset. I've never stayed out all night before. I expect they'll all be looking for me, and calling, and setting out dishes of milk. My sisters will be crying. They won't know what to do without me."

The black kitten cocked her head and looked inquiring.

"I don't know just exactly where my

house is," Alexander said. "I got turned around while I was exploring. Two huge trucks ran over me. And then some huge dogs hunted me. But I escaped!"

He looked about. There was nothing to see but trees, and trees behind the trees, and snow beginning to fall among the trees.

"I'm lost," he said at last, in a small voice.

"Me!" said the black kitten cheerfully, and pounced on his tail. Then she trotted off through the trees and the falling snow, her wings folded, her tail held high. And Alexander followed her.

3

IT WAS LATE EVENING again when at last, footsore and starving hungry, the two kittens came in sight of a big old barn. High in the front wall were holes that had been made for pigeons to fly in and out of. Alexander blinked when he saw another winged cat fly out of one of those pigeonholes— and then another—and then two more. The littlest one came swooping towards them, calling to the others, "Look! It's Jane! She's walking! With a strange kitten!"

And all four of the winged cats came flying about poor Alexander's head, until he put his paws over it and flattened himself on the ground.

When he finally looked up, he saw the black kitten joyously flying loop-the-loops over the barn. Then she dived straight down into a bowl of kibbles.

Beside him sat a handsome young tabby cat with tabby wings. "I'm Roger," the cat said, "and we are the Catwings. Don't be afraid!"

"I'm not afraid," Alexander said fiercely. "I am Alexander Furby."

"I'm glad to know you, Alexander. Will you come and have some dinner with us?" Roger said.

Alexander did not need to be asked twice.

When dinner was over, he was so tired and so full that all he could do was waddle after the black kitten into the barn. On the floor was a pile of sweet dry hay, and in the hay the two kittens curled up together, purred once, and fell fast asleep.

The next day, Alexander learned all the Catwings' names: handsome Roger, thoughtful Thelma, kind James, who limped a little on one wing, small Harriet, and his

own special friend, the black kitten, their youngest sister, Jane.

It seemed sad to Alexander that Jane had not been able to tell him her own name. While she was off flying about somewhere, he asked Thelma about her.

"Well, Alexander," Thelma said, "we're the only cats with wings in all the world, so far as we know. We four older ones were born in the city, underneath a dumpster. Our dear mother, like you, had no wings. But she was very wise, and as soon as we could fly well, she told us to fly far away. She knew that if we were caught, the people of the city would make shows of us, and put us in cages, and we would never have any freedom. By great good fortune we came to this place, where our friends Hank and Susan look after us. They take care that no one knows about us."

"They are your Caretakers," said Alexander.

"Yes," said Thelma. "Well, once James and Harriet returned to the city to visit our dear mother. They found our street in ruins, but hiding in an attic was a young black kitten with wings."

"It was Jane!" said Alexander.

Thelma nodded. "Our little sister, Jane. She was all alone, and the building she was in was about to be destroyed. They rescued her. After they found our mother and visited with her, they brought Jane home to our farm. But little Jane has never said a word, except *Me*, and when she is frightened, she says, *Hate!* We think something terrible happened to her when she was a young kitten, separated from our mother."

"When she was hiding in the attic?" Alexander asked.

"Yes," said Thelma. "She won't even come up to the loft of the barn, where we sleep. It must remind her of that attic. That's why she sleeps in the hay downstairs. She's well, and seems happy enough. But she can't speak."

"She's very brave. She rescued me," Alexander said.

"I'm very glad she did," said Thelma, and she gently pushed him down and washed him quite hard all over, just as if she were his own mother.

"Thelma," Alexander said, "my mother will be worried about me."

"We've talked about that," said Thelma. "Susan and Hank will be here soon. Wait till you meet them!"

And very soon over the hill came a boy and a girl, with a can full of milk and a bag full of kibbles. All the Catwings came swooping about them, and perched on their shoulders and heads and hands and noses, and purred at them, and Susan and Hank laughed at the Catwings and petted them and threw kibbles in the air for them to catch. But then they saw Alexander.

"Look!" they said.

Alexander came towards them rather

shyly, waving his tail. It was golden and plumy, like his mother's tail.

"Oh!" said Susan. "Oh, the poor little kitten! He doesn't have any wings!"

Her brother, Hank, laughed. "Most kittens don't, Sooz," he said.

Susan was already holding Alexander and petting him. Alexander was purring madly.

"Listen, Sooz," Hank said. "You know Mother has been saying she'd like to have a cat. But she can't have one of the Catwings, because visitors might see it. If this is a stray kitten . . ."

So Alexander found himself being carried on Susan's shoulder over the hill to the farmhouse where the children lived.

There the children's mother greeted him. "Oh," she said, "what a wonderful tail! What a wonderful kitten!" And she scratched him under the chin.

"What an intelligent woman," Alexander thought.

"But where do you think he came from?"

the children's mother asked. Nobody knew. And Alexander could not tell them, since cats and human beings don't talk the same way.

He settled down at the farmhouse, where he was treated very well, though there were no sardines and no feather beds. At night he could sleep with Susan or with Hank. But he was expected to live outdoors during the day, and to catch mice when he grew up.

Every day he trotted over the hill to the old barn and played with Jane and the other Catwings. He was very happy. But he did think about his mother and father and sisters, and so one day, when a red car drove into the farmhouse yard, he grew very excited and came running with his plumy tail waving.

Out of the little red car stepped the Owner.

"Is that you, Alexander?" he said.

Alexander purred and rubbed his head on the Owner's leg. Then he danced off to the front door, for he wanted him to meet Hank and Susan and their mother and father.

The Owner came in and talked a while with the children's mother and father. The children's mother was polite, but her voice trembled a little when she said, "I have become very fond of him, but he is your kitten."

"His sisters have an excellent new home," said the Owner. "I can only come to my country house now and then. Of course Mr. and Mrs. Furby will live there. But if you could keep Alexander, I would be truly grateful."

"Oh, I should love to keep him!" cried the children's mother.

Alexander looked from one to the other,

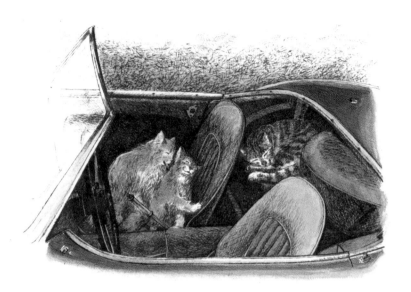

and purred extremely loudly, so that they both laughed.

Every now and then the Owner came by in his red car with Mr. and Mrs. Furby, so that Alexander could see his mother and father again.

Mr. Furby was usually asleep in the back seat, but Mrs. Furby always washed Alexander's face carefully and told him to be her own wonderful boy.

"Of course," said Alexander.

4

LIFE WAS GOOD at Overhill Farm. Alexander was growing fast. His tail was magnificent. He had nearly caught two mice. Every day he and Jane played all about the old barn and in the woods.

James taught him how to fish in the creek, and Roger taught him to stalk. Thelma told him hair-raising stories about the city where she and the other Catwings had been born. And little Harriet played hide-and-pounce every evening with him and Jane.

But sometimes Alexander sat with his plumy tail around his paws and thought. He remembered how he had left home intending to do wonderful things.

All he had done was get nearly run over by a truck, chased by a dog, stuck in a tree, and lost. Jane had saved him and brought him to this happy home. It was Jane who had done the wonderful thing.

What wonderful thing could he possibly do for Jane?

What could an ordinary cat do for a cat with wings?

He sat with his tail around his paws and watched Jane soaring high, high above him, playing with the swallows in the sunlight of spring.

He went and ate some kibbles—he was always hungry these days—and then trotted to their favorite play-place near the woods and called, "Jane!"

She came swooping down on her beautiful black wings, landed beside him lightly on her little black paws, and smiled at him.

"Jane," said Alexander.

"Purr," said Jane.

"Jane, you can talk."

Jane stopped purring. She lashed her tail.

"I know you were terribly frightened when you were little," Alexander said. "Thelma told me how you and your mother lost each other, and how you hid all alone in the attic of a deserted building and had nothing to eat. And then machines tore down the building. It must have been awful. But there must have been something even worse—something so bad you can't talk about it—something so bad you can't talk *at all*. But if you don't talk, Jane, how will we ever know what it was?"

Jane said nothing and did not look at Alexander. She began to stalk a grasshopper in the tall grass.

"You showed me that I could get down from that pine tree," Alexander said. "I know you can get away from the bad thing. But I can't help if I don't know what it was. You have to tell me, Jane."

Jane went on stalking the grasshopper. Alexander put a paw on her tail so that she had to stop. She growled at him.

"You can growl all you like," he said. "I'm going to stand on your tail till you talk to me!"

Jane growled again and bit Alexander, hard enough that it hurt.

"Don't!" Alexander said. "Don't bite!

Talk! Tell me. Tell me what frightened you in that attic!"

"HATE!" Jane said, with her eyes round and staring, and her fur all on end. "HATE! HATE!"

"Hate what? What did you hate?"

Jane's back arched and she stared at Alexander with such rage and terror that his fur, too, stood on end. "Jane!" he said. "Tell me!"

"Rats," Jane said in a strange, hissing voice. "Rats. There—were—RATS—there."

She began to shiver all over, and Alexander curled himself around her to comfort her.

"Rats, much bigger than me," Jane said in a hoarse, weak voice that grew stronger as she spoke. "They were hungry, too. They hunted me. All the time. They would wait. They whispered to each other. I couldn't get to the water in the gutter. They'd wait there to catch me. I could only

fly a little. I hid in the rafters. But they climbed up there. I found a place, an old mouse nest in a box. They couldn't get in there. But they waited outside it, and whispered. I didn't know what to do. I would call to my mother. But the rats would answer." And Jane hid her face in Alexander's warm, furry side.

He washed her back and her neck and both her ears with his rough pink tongue, and purred to her. "It's all right. You got away from them. You don't ever have to be afraid of them again. You have wings, Jane. You can fly anywhere."

"I love you, Alexander," Jane said.

"I love you, Jane," Alexander said.

"I wanted to talk! I just couldn't."

"Let's go show the others," said Alexander.

They hurried off, Alexander trotting along with his tail high, and Jane loop-the-looping overhead, to the old barn.

"Thelma! Roger! Harriet! James!"

"Yes, Alexander," said the brothers and sisters, who had been asleep in the loft. They came popping out of the pigeonholes. "What's up?"

"That wasn't me calling you," said Alexander.

"Me!" said Jane. "It was me! I can talk!"

They all gathered around her while she explained.

"I was afraid if I talked, the only thing I could say would be the bad thing—the rats. And then they'd be real again. But I know it's all right, and I can talk. Because Alexander showed me."

"If a rat ever came here," said little Harriet, "it would find out what an air raid is!"

"We've got to pay another visit to Mother," said James. "It will make her so happy when you talk to her, Jane."

"Alexander," said Roger very solemnly, "you are wonderful."

"Yes!" said Jane. "He's wonderful!"

"I know," said Alexander.